For Kevin – Our Crazy Diamond.
Shine Bright x

ONE

I hear Mum laughing as soon as I walk into the house. To be fair, the sound would be pretty hard to miss. Mum has the kind of laugh that can wake the dead – shrill and high pitched. It's the type that can shatter glass. Mum's friend Maggie must be here again. *Great!*

"No, Maggie!" Mum says loudly. "It's not like that at all!"

I throw my school bag down and stroll along the hall to find her. Freddie is sitting at the kitchen table and looks up at me right away. He is always so excited when I come home, like I'm the best thing ever.

"Vee!" Freddie cries. He throws down his crayon and runs over to me. I am bowled over by a sticky four year old. I can smell the sweet scents of coconut shampoo from his messy hair and the chocolate that is smeared all around his face.

"Have you been eating biscuits again?" I say, and peer down at my school skirt, which is now covered with dark handprints.

Nice! I need to stick it in the wash now.

"Mum said I can!" Freddie says.

"It's a treat!" Mum shouts from the conservatory. "Don't moan at him, Vee. He's been so good!"

I pull out a wet wipe from the pack on the table and rub at Freddie's dirty face. "You'll attract wasps and flies," I tell him. "And you shouldn't be eating biscuits at this time – you won't eat your dinner."

"I still will ..." Freddie says. "I promise."

Mum is laughing again. Her voice floats over to me. "Sometimes, Maggie," she says to her friend, "I wonder who the mother is here."

She isn't the only one.

I wander over to her. The conservatory is basically Mum's studio, where she cuts people's hair and sometimes does their nails. She has put proper hairdressing chairs in there, lined up facing the mirrors on the wall. There are expensive blinds hanging at the windows to stop it getting too hot. She even has a small table with a selection of dull magazines and trashy books.

Maggie is one of Mum's regular customers, as well as her best friend. She's currently sitting under a dryer with her head plastered in bright silver foils that are glinting in the sun. Both Maggie and Mum are drinking wine. No surprise there then.

"Why are you so grumpy?" Mum asks me, and sits back in her chair. "Have you had a bad day at school or something?"

"No. Not at all." I glare at her wine glass. "Isn't it a bit early for that?"

Mum's bright lips curl into a smile, but I can see that her eyes are much cooler, warning me off. "It's just one glass, Violet." She uses my full name and flaps a hand at me. "You need to loosen up a bit."

I shake my head at her. *Whatever.* To be fair, I can't see a half-empty wine bottle anywhere, so perhaps this time they actually *are* just having one glass.

It is no big deal.

"I'm going upstairs," I tell Mum. "I have homework to do."

"OK, but would you mind putting Freddie's tea on in a bit?" Mum says. "I'll be busy with Maggie for a while yet."

Maggie glances over at me as if to apologise and then looks away again fast.

"No, that's fine," I reply. "I'll make a start on my English at least."

"You really are an angel," Mum says. "Wasn't I just saying that, Maggie – what an angel Violet is? I don't know where I'd be without her."

I walk away before I can hear the answer.

One thing you need to know about my mum is that she always takes good care of herself. I guess she has to because of her job. You only have to walk into our bathroom to see the amount of beauty products and make-up that she has. Hardly any of it is mine. I can't be bothered with it all really. But Mum is different. She spends ages at the mirror, curling her long dark hair, smoothing foundation onto her tanned skin and taking time to apply her false lashes.

She looks amazing afterwards – pretty, glamorous and confident. That's just how she is, my mum. She always tells me, "You have to look good, Vee. You have to give a good impression at all times." Then she will raise her eyebrows at my messy hair and pale skin and beg me to use some of her products.

"I can't understand why you're not more like me," Mum often moans. "You could be, you know. You could be really stunning if you just let yourself."

And I can never answer her, because I don't know why stuff like make-up doesn't interest me. I can't really explain to her why I find it heavy and uncomfortable. I know that I am very different to Mum. I am the quiet one – the class swot who dreams of being a lawyer one day. I'm the worrier who can never be confident.

It isn't like that for Mum. She has always been strong, funny and in control.

At least that's what I always used to believe. But then, I used to believe in fairy stories too, until I realised that not everything ends in a happy ever after.

Much later, I put Freddie to bed after I've fed him and given him a bath. Mum and Maggie are still drinking downstairs but have now moved into the living room. Mum has decided to put her music on. It's some really annoying rubbish from the eighties with screechy vocals.

"It's too loud," Freddie moans, pulling his duvet over his head.

"It's OK," I soothe him. "I'll close your door. You'll soon be asleep."

"I wish Dad was here," he mutters. "It was so much better when Dad was here."

I blink, trying to think of the right things to say. Freddie's dad, Steve, left us nearly a year ago. That's when everything started to unravel. Now Steve lives miles away with his new girlfriend. I sometimes wonder if he even remembers we still exist.

"Mum will stop soon," I say. "Just you wait."

But we both know she won't. Mum does this all the time. If I complain, she'll just say that I'm trying to spoil her fun. I'm not in the mood for an argument, so instead I slip into my own room and try not to think about it.

Hopefully it *will* be over soon. The only thing I can do is wait until she falls asleep and then I can creep downstairs and turn the music off myself.

On my desk, the rest of my English homework is waiting for me. I sit for a bit, trying hard to focus, but all I can hear are Mum's shrieks of laughter from downstairs. And then a bit later comes her high-pitched singing – out of tune and piercing my brain. It's impossible to focus.

"Please be quiet," I whisper.

The words in front of me are swimming around, almost jumping off the page. I can't focus at all. Frustrated, I push the papers aside and lie down on my bed instead, ramming my pillow over my head. After a while I hear the front door slam. Maggie has gone home at last. That's something at least.

But the music stays on. Booming and relentless.

I know that Mum will keep going for a good while yet. This has become the new normal for us.

TWO

My alarm goes off at seven and I quickly get up and get myself washed. Then I attempt to drag Freddie out of bed. He isn't very good at getting up. In fact, most days it's like he is glued to the sheets.

"Fred – come on!" I groan, whipping off his duvet. "We're going to be late."

I really can't afford for that to happen again. School are already on my case about my attendance.

Mum's bedroom door is slightly ajar, so I poke my head around the gap. The room is dimly lit and I can see that she is spread out on the bed, her face pressed into the pillows. The air smells musty and thick.

"Mum!" I say loudly. "We have to get up. It's seven-thirty already."

She groans but barely moves.

"Mum! You have to get up!" I repeat, and pad round to the side of her bed. One of her eyes opens. It is sticky with gunky make-up that she hasn't bothered to take off. The pillow is smeared with yellow foundation.

"Mum – we have to leave in half an hour," I remind her. "You have to wake up now."

I am getting pretty used to doing this frustrating wake-up call. I can hear Freddie crashing around in the room next door as he attempts to get dressed.

"Vee – I'm not well," Mum groans, rubbing her head. "I'm really sorry … You'll have to take Freddie to school today."

"What?" I stare back at her, rage burning inside me. "How can I?"

Our schools are both on the other side of town, and Freddie's starts just a few minutes before mine. Mum knows that if I take Freddie to school first I won't be on time myself.

"Mum. I can't be late. If I am, they will give me a detention."

I can hear Mr Anderson, my head of year, now. "Violet – this is an important year for you. You can't afford to keep rolling into school after the bell. It shows lack of effort and a bad attitude ..."

Mr Anderson knows nothing.

"You have to drive us," I say. "Please, Mum."

"I'm in no state to drive," she mutters. "It wouldn't be safe."

To be fair, she is probably right. Her eyes are red raw and she stinks of wine – like someone has tipped an entire bottle over her and rubbed it into her skin. I wonder how much she drank last night. More than normal.

"I'm sorry," Mum says. "Take some money from my bag. Get a bus. You'll be a bit early then. Freddie can wait with his teacher."

"You know Freddie hates buses."

"Just hold his hand tight. He'll be fine. He'll have to be ..." Mum's talking slowly, her words muffled. "It's just one day, Vee. That's all."

"Mum—"

She nestles herself back into bed and pulls the covers up over her chin. "I need to rest, Vee – please."

"OK. Whatever," I say, and stomp out of the room, leaving the door wide open. I am hoping the stale smell might escape out that way. Even if part of me feels like she deserves to put up with the stink. It is her fault after all.

Freddie has got dressed fast. He is good like that. He meets me downstairs, where I quickly make him some breakfast. I have already loaded the dirty glasses Mum left out into the dishwasher and whipped the empty wine bottles into the recycling bin. I don't want Freddie to see them and worry. There were five bottles this time. That has to be a record.

"Is Mum OK?" Freddie asks, his eyes wide. "Why is she still in bed?"

"She just has a bit of a headache," I tell him. "She needs to sleep a bit longer."

He nods, milk dribbling from his lips. "She has headaches a lot ..."

"Yeah," I agree. "She does."

Mum's handbag is lying open on the kitchen table. It is a huge bulky thing. She calls it her suitcase because she carries so much stuff in it, like her hairbrushes and clips. Her large black purse is poking out of the top. I reach to grab it. I almost don't spot what is hidden underneath.

Almost.

But my fingers touch glass as I pull out the purse. I can't help but peer in closer.

A bottle.

Gently I turn it around onto its front.

It is a small bottle of vodka, nestled there among Mum's hair bands and keys.

And it is already half empty.

Freddie isn't happy as we wait at the bus stop.

"I don't like buses," he says. "You know I don't. They are loud and scary and I might fall over."

Freddie's fear of buses started when he was two. We had been on a packed bus going to town, so we had to stand. Then the bus braked suddenly and Freddie fell forward and hit his head on a pole. He was OK, just bruised and a bit shaken – but the incident has put him off buses for life.

"Mum should take me," Freddie mutters. "In the car. Like normal."

"Well, Mum can't," I say.

Or won't.

I pull Freddie towards me. "Look, I can hold you tight. I'll keep you safe. I'm good at it."

I try not to feel too angry. After all, this is only the second time it has happened this month. Normally Mum is able to get out of bed and drive. But the thought of that hidden bottle is tearing into me.

Maybe it isn't Mum's? Maybe she found it or is keeping it for someone?

Maybe it was a gift – a present from one of her clients?

Maybe it is just really old?

The bus pulls up and we step on. Annoyingly, it's already a few minutes late and it is packed, so Freddie and I have to squeeze in. We end up standing by the front, sandwiched between a mum with her buggy and a woman talking loudly on her phone. Freddie shuffles himself next to me and keeps his eyes focused on the floor. He looks very pale. My thoughts keep on tumbling.

Is Mum drinking more than normal? Is she hiding it from me?

My head is hurting just thinking about it. I try to focus on the passing roads instead, watching as the bus hurtles across town. It is another miserable day and the rain is streaking against the window in misty drifts.

"Will Mum be better later?" Freddie asks suddenly.

"I think so," I reply. I know that Mum has appointments booked in today, so she'll need to get out of bed soon.

"Will she be picking me up from school?" Freddie asks, his face pinched with worry. "I don't want her to be late again."

"Of course she will, Freddie. You know she always does. I'm sure she will be on time."

I smile at him and squeeze his hand. Mum is normally fine in the afternoons. At least that is something I am confident about.

The stupid bus arrives late, but Ness meets me by the school gates as always. I am so grateful she is there. There is something reassuring about the sight of my best friend waiting for me, even if she does look a bit stressed. Ness has been my friend for so long that I honestly can't imagine being without her. I can still remember sitting with her in the sandpit at playschool.

"I'm so sorry," I say, seeing Ness's worried face. "I had to take Freddie in first."

"How come you had Freddie?" Ness frowns at me. "It's already ten to nine – we'd better get a move on or we'll be in trouble."

We walk quickly to the school entrance. I can already see Mr Anderson standing there with the late register in his hands. My stomach drops. Why does he have to be on duty today?

"I'm so sorry," I say to Ness. "I don't want to get you in trouble too. Mum isn't feeling well. You shouldn't have waited for me."

Ness shrugs. "I'm only missing tutor group and who cares about that anyway?"

Mr Anderson stands looming over us. He is scarily tall, with a huge nose that reminds me of a bird. I can picture him bending over and pecking us, as if we were annoying little bugs. I know he sees me as some sort of bug. A bug he doesn't like very much.

"The bell rang five minutes ago," Mr Anderson barks, his eyes scanning me. "What's the excuse this time?"

I feel flustered. "I had to take my brother to school, sir," I explain. "He goes to Merrymead, so it's hard to get back here in time ..."

He sighs and turns to Ness. "And I suppose you had to hold her hand, did you?"

Ness's cheeks flush pink. She hates any kind of confrontation. "I ... I just wanted to wait for her, sir," Ness says. "I was worried ..."

I look at her and feel a glow of shame. Ness doesn't need to wait for me, of course, but I know she likes to. She hates walking into school on her own. That is just Ness.

"Well, it's a shame you did, as now you will both have late codes," Mr Anderson says. His gaze floats back to me and he adds, *"Again."* His glare pierces right into me. "You know that means a detention tonight, Violet? I trust I won't be spoiling any of your plans?"

"No, sir," I say. "Not at all."

I can't do anything but smile weakly and accept it. It isn't like anyone here would ever understand.

The fact is, no one would.

Ness grabs my arm on the way to tutor group. "I hate him so much," she mutters.

I nod – *me too.* "But, Ness – you don't have to wait for me," I tell her. "You knew I was going to be late. You should have gone in ..."

Ness shakes her head lightly. "No. No ... I don't like to do that."

I glance over and see that she is twisting her fingers. She always does that when she is nervous.

"I don't know what difference me being with you makes," I say, and half laugh.

Ness shrugs. "I dunno. I just feel less anxious, I guess. I can tell myself that everything will be OK."

I drop my head. This feels like a lot of pressure. How can I make everything OK for someone else? I can barely make my own life function properly.

"Vee – are you sure everything is OK?" Ness asks, her voice soft.

I hesitate. For a split second, I look at Ness's worried expression and I really want to talk. I do. I want to tell her exactly what is going on in my mind.

No, actually, I'm not OK – it's my mum. She got drunk again last night. And no, it's not normal. She keeps doing this. She keeps drinking and then acting like everything is fine. But it's not, is it? How is this fine?

But instead I stare back at Ness's wide, clear eyes. I know what she would say. Ness, with her overthinking mind and kind nature. Ness, who has hard-working and loving parents – to whom she tells everything. She would want to try to help me, of course, but she'd also end up causing a whole load of trouble. Mum would never, ever forgive me if I got other people involved.

No. I can't risk that. I can't risk anyone else finding out what is going on.

I can't risk hurting Mum.

"I'm fine, Ness. Honestly," I say, and flash her my brightest grin. "I'm just tired. That's all. I didn't sleep too well last night."

At least that isn't a lie.

I try to ignore the tiny frown on Ness's face. She nods and turns away.

And I try to ignore the worried thoughts that are now overcrowding my brain.

It'll be OK, I tell myself – I keep telling myself. *It'll be OK. Mum will be fine later. She has to be.*

This is just another little blip.

THREE

How long do blips last for? Days? Weeks? Longer?

Surely we are at the end of ours now. It can't go on for much longer.

I always thought that blips were meant to be short, small things. They were meant to be like tiny bumps in the road, not waves in an endless ocean.

So is this really a blip?

Or is it something a whole lot worse?

I push open the front door when I get home from school and wait for a second, just listening. I can hear voices inside, but I need to know if they

are the right ones. From the back of the house I
hear Freddie laughing. And then a louder, more
familiar, booming voice.

"I'm coming to get you!"

My heart flips with relief. It's Grandad! He
and Nan have come for dinner as usual.

Everything is going to be all right.

I walk into the house feeling a million times
lighter. The TV is on low in the living room and
I can see Freddie running around the kitchen
island. Grandad is chasing him as if in slow
motion, with his arms held up high and putting on
his silly "troll" voice. They both race outside into
the garden, Freddie squealing. It is so good to see
Grandad happy and active like this, but part of
me is still frozen with worry. Only a few months
ago he had a minor heart attack. Grandad is
much better now, but he still needs to be careful.
Should he really be running around like this?
What if he gets ill again?

"I'm going to get you!" Grandad is yelling.

"No ... No ..." Freddie replies with joy.

I shake away my fears and smile weakly.
I can't let myself think like that. Not now.

"Hi! I'm home!" I call out.

"In here, sweetie!" Mum calls back.

Mum and Nan are sitting at the dining-room table. I glance over and see that they are both drinking coffee. Mum is dressed in jeans and her favourite white T-shirt, which makes her skin look more golden than ever. She has swept her hair up into a loose ponytail and her make-up is perfect. She looks relaxed, healthy and pretty much gorgeous.

"Mum – are you feeling better?" I ask.

A tiny frown appears on her face as if she is trying to remember. "Oh – I'm all good, honey," Mum says, taking a small sip of her drink. I notice the tiniest shake in her hands. She quickly puts them together on her lap, out of sight.

"Have you not been well, Kathy?" Nan asks sharply.

Mum giggles softly. "I just had a bit of a headache this morning. That's all. Nothing much." She turns her attention to me to ask, "Aren't you a bit late home?"

I slump down in the chair beside her. "Well – yes, I got a detention this morning for being late. Remember? I told you I would."

"Oh yes." Mum pinches her lips together. "I'm sorry."

Nan looks over at me, concerned. "Why were you late, Violet?"

"I had to take Freddie to school because Mum was ill," I tell her.

"But surely the school understood that?" Nan says, and shakes her head. I can see she is getting cross. She turns to Mum. "Shouldn't you call them? It's hardly fair that the school punished Violet for helping you out."

"But, Nan—" I start to explain.

I stop as I catch Mum's stare. It is as cool as ice. She gives her head a slight shake. Mum knows what I am going to say – that this isn't the first time. That this keeps happening and the school is getting fed up with my excuses. I'm not sure that they even believe me any more.

But of course Mum doesn't want Nan to know that.

"It's OK, Mum," she says to Nan, lightly touching her hand. "I'll call the school in the morning. I'll explain everything. It's my mess after all."

Mum's gaze falls back on me. She is smiling still, but we both know that she isn't happy.

We also both know that she has no intention of calling the school. She never does.

It is just another one of her lies.

Nan and Grandad leave soon after dinner. I am trying to get some homework done at the dining table and Freddie is flopped out on the sofa, exhausted, watching TV. His face is red and sweaty from running about too much. Mum sighs heavily and starts crashing around the kitchen, moaning that there is no food left.

"I have nothing for our breakfast tomorrow," she moans.

"Maybe you should go shopping then?" I point out.

"Funny …" Mum mutters back. "I don't have the time. You'll have to make do with jam on toast. There's a bit of bread left."

"What about you?" I say, looking up.

"It's fine. I don't eat much in the day."

Mum never eats much in the evening either.

I half watch her as she moves around the room, cleaning the surfaces, putting stuff away. She seems slower today, like she is tired.

"Are you really OK?" I ask.

"I'm fine," Mum says. She walks over to the fridge and pulls out a bottle of wine. "A glass of this will help."

I stare hard at her. "Mum. Is that a good idea?"

"Yes. It is, actually. And one glass won't hurt anyone," she scoffs. "After the day I've had, it's my reward."

Drinking is always Mum's reward. Like, if she has a busy day, she says, "Oh, I deserve this drink." If someone has upset her, she opens up the wine and tells me that it makes her "feel better". She treats drinking like she has earned it, like how Freddie argues he deserves his sweets for being good.

I watch as Mum pours the glass of wine and takes a long slug. She sighs with satisfaction.

"So what kind of day did you have?" I ask bluntly. "Why was it so bad?"

Mum peers over her glass at me like she'd forgotten I was there and says, "What?"

"You said you deserved the wine because of your bad day. So what happened?"

She shrugs. "Oh – you know. I had that awful headache when I woke up, so I ended up late for a client. I guess they weren't very happy about that. And then someone else cancelled this afternoon." Mum takes another sip. No, not a sip, a gulp. "I guess it was just one of those days."

"I guess," I reply.

I can hear the cackling laughter of Freddie's cartoons coming from the other room. Mum slugs the last of her wine. "Don't worry, Vee. It will be a better day tomorrow, I'm sure."

I stare at her. My eyes burn into her. Mum doesn't flinch. She just smiles back at me calmly.

"The trouble with you, Vee, is that you worry too much," Mum says softly, shaking her head.

No – the trouble with me is that I have you for a mum ...

It's no wonder I worry all the time. Who could blame me?

What else *can* I do but worry?

Mum wasn't always like this. *We* weren't always like this. There was a time when we were a "happy family" in every sense of the word. Of course, that was when Steve was still here. Mum was different around him. It was like she had a light inside that was always shining. She laughed a lot and she didn't get stressed at all. I only remember her having wine occasionally with dinner, and mostly just one glass.

And then it all changed ...

When Steve left us, it was like a huge boulder had just hurtled through our home, leaving behind this massive hole. Freddie was so upset and kept crying for his dad, asking when he'd come back. I didn't say it, but I felt the same.

Steve might not be my actual dad, but he was the nearest thing I ever had to one. I never even knew my own father. He left when Mum was pregnant with me. Steve was part of our lives for years, and now – well, now there is just something missing. Steve seemed happy with us, so what went wrong? I used to ask the question all the time, but no one wanted to tell me the answer.

Mum changed the most out of all of us. At first, it was like she was in a trance, and she didn't really talk to any of us. In fact, she was not really "there" at all. Then Mum started getting upset and crying a lot. That's when Maggie started to come around in the evenings and they would sit up late at night, talking and crying.

That was the first time I heard Mum say it as she poured herself a large glass of red wine – "I really need this. I need this, after what he did to me."

It became a regular thing then: the wine bottles in the kitchen, the glasses piling up in the sink, Mum's loud voice drifting upstairs as we tried to sleep.

At first it was OK – it was better than the shouting that happened just before Steve walked out. It was better than the long silences that took over afterwards. Drinking seemed to help her, after all.

Mum seemed to be happy again.

At least – that's what I believed at the beginning, anyway.

Later on that evening, Mum is getting more wound up. She has had a few glasses of wine by now and has been trying to call Steve for the last hour with no luck.

"Just answer the bloody phone!" Mum screams. Then she throws her mobile across the room.

I take Freddie's hand and quickly lead him out of the room. I hear the smash of something being thrown at the wall, and I guess it is the picture of Mum and Steve together. She's only just fixed it after the last time she flung it across the room.

Freddie rubs his nose. He always does that when he is scared or anxious. "Why is Mum so angry?" he whispers. "Why does she keep shouting like that?"

"I think she's just tired," I lie.

I lead Freddie upstairs, trying to ignore the sound of Mum letting out another angry roar. Then she swears loudly several times and we both flinch.

"I hate this," Freddie says.

"Me too," I say.

"Who is she shouting at?" he asks, chewing his bottom lip. "Is it Daddy?"

I sigh, not sure what to tell him. "I think so. I think she wants to talk to him but he's not answering his phone."

"Why isn't he?"

"He's probably just busy, Freddie," I say. "Or his phone is turned off." I know that is not what Mum believes. Mum hates the fact that Steve rarely answers her calls now. She says that he does it on purpose. She thinks that he is ignoring her and trying to wind her up.

"He's a coward," she says. "He's too busy with his new woman – Chloe."

Mum spits out her name like it is poison. She doesn't see how it upsets Freddie, who actually really likes his dad's new girlfriend.

Steve probably doesn't want to speak to Mum because he knows what she'll be like, I think. *He knows that she will be drunk and swear at him, especially by the evening. She will say nasty things to him and then regret it. Then she will cry and beg for Steve's forgiveness. Like she always does. Then she will plead for him to come home.*

I know this is the case because Mum has been doing it for months now.

"Does Mummy hate Daddy?" Freddie asks quietly as I sort out his pyjamas.

"No," I say, stroking his baby-soft hair. "She doesn't hate him at all. Mum just gets silly sometimes and says things that she doesn't mean. It's just because she's hurting, I think."

"Is that why she says horrible things? Like bad words?" Freddie pouts. "I hate it when she does that."

"Me too," I say. "I'm sorry she does that. I think she forgets you're there."

I think she forgets we're both there ...

Freddie leans up against me and I pull him into a tight hug. He is so small, so delicate. I press my nose into his hair and breathe in the familiar scent of his coconut shampoo. It is so comforting.

"I love you, Freddie," I whisper, my words muffled. "And I'll always be here for you. Just remember, I love you to the moon and back."

My skin prickles. Mum used to say this to us over and over again whenever we were upset or needed a hug. "Don't cry. Everything will be OK. I love you to the moon and back. I always will."

"And the moon is very far away, isn't it?" Freddie whispers.

"Really far ..." I say. "Too far to imagine."

Freddie's fingers curl around mine and grip me tight.

"I'll always be here for you," I tell him.

And I mean it.

FOUR

Saturdays used to be my favourite day. They were always long, lazy days flopped in front of the TV. Sometimes we would go to the park or swimming in the afternoons. Most evenings we would chill out in front of a film eating big bags of popcorn or drinking huge mugs of frothy hot chocolate. This was when it was me, Mum, Freddie and Steve, of course – when he was still around.

They used to be our family days.

Now Saturdays aren't so great. They are fragments of what they used to be.

It is just before midday when Mum finally drags herself out of bed. I have already sorted out Freddie and settled him in front of the TV, yet again. I try not to make any sarcastic comments when Mum slops in. She doesn't look so good today. Her hair is un-brushed and she still has traces of yesterday's make-up. The dark smudges look like shadows dotted under her eyes. She doesn't speak to me or Freddie. She just walks into the kitchen and starts to slam the cupboards in there, like she is looking for something. I wonder if she has noticed that I cleaned up all her mess from last night.

I seriously doubt it.

"Are you all right?" I call out to her.

"Yeah, I just ..." Mum's voice drifts away. "I'm fine. I need painkillers."

I hear the tap run as she gets herself some water. I guess she has another headache.

Mum's work mobile on the living-room table starts ringing. She has two phones. Her personal one, which is bright pink and very "blingy", and her work one, which is more expensive and for setting up appointments. I shout out to her.

"Mum. You've got a call."

Mum stands in the doorway. She looks panicked. "Vee – can you answer it and tell them

I'm ill? Please. I can't work today. I just can't."
Mum runs a hand through her messed-up hair.

I look at her, shocked. "Mum, you never cancel appointments!"

This is Mum's business that she has spent years building up. Mum never messes people around. She knows that she has a good reputation and always says she will do whatever it takes to keep it. I've known Mum to work even when she is really tired or ill – she just hates letting people down.

"Please," Mum begs. "Just today. You don't know how rough I feel. I can't face leaving the house."

Reluctantly, I take the call. I don't recognise the woman's voice on the other end. It's somebody called April, who is expecting Mum to cut and blow-dry her hair at her house. Mum doesn't only work from home, she also cuts and styles hair at people's houses – especially if they have a special occasion that day.

"She is meant to be here now. Where is she?" April barks. "I'm starting to worry."

"I'm really sorry. My mum isn't feeling very well," I say as politely as I can. "Can we rearrange the appointment?"

"And you're only telling me this now?" April says. "Surely I should've had a call earlier this morning at the very least? I'm meant to be going out tonight. My hair will look awful now."

"I'm so sorry," I tell her.

"So you should be. I'll have to go into town now and try to get a slot at a proper salon. Tell your mum I'll never be using her again and I'll be telling my friends to do the same."

April cuts off the call and I am left staring at the phone like it has stung me.

Mum walks into the room. She is clutching her glass of water. "I'm so sorry, Vee," she says flatly. "I stayed up too late last night doing my accounts. I just can't face cutting hair today. I wouldn't do a good job of it."

"You were trying to call Steve last night," I snap back. I certainly don't remember seeing her with any paperwork.

Mum holds my gaze. Her eyes are rimmed with red. "Yes, I called him too," she says. "So what? He owes me money. I need to talk to him about it. That's part of my accounting."

"You shouldn't be shouting down the phone at him though," I tell her. "It scares Freddie."

"Well, I'm sorry," Mum says slowly and very coldly. "But maybe Freddie needs to realise that his dad isn't such a hero. Steve left us completely in the lurch. Look at what he did. Moving up north with his new woman without a care. What use is he to us? Look at the damage he's done ..."

Mum takes a gulp of her drink and wipes her mouth with the back of her hand. I notice it shaking again. "We're on our own now, Vee," Mum says. "So to be honest I'd appreciate a bit of your support."

"I do support you."

"Really?" Mum's eyes burrow into mine. "Because most of the time it feels more like you're judging me."

We always go to Nan and Grandad's on Saturday afternoon now. But today Mum insists that she needs to rest and tells me and Freddie to go without her. So we leave her lying on the sofa, still in her pyjamas, watching some naff property programme on TV.

"Are you sure you'll be OK on your own?" I ask.

"Of course I will. Stop fussing," Mum says, flapping her hand at me. "A few hours of peace on my own is just what I need."

Mum doesn't know that I have already checked the fridge and all the cupboards in the kitchen. I can't find any alcohol, which I have to take as a good sign. Mum isn't dressed to go out and doesn't look like she is in any mood to leave the house. So that means she is going to be OK today. She isn't going to have a drink.

And maybe Mum is right. Maybe all she needs is a rest from everything. It might help to clear her head and get her back on track.

"Come on, Freddie," I say, tugging his arm. "Let's go."

It isn't a long walk to Nan and Grandad's. We just have to walk across the park opposite our house and then after a few more streets we are more or less there. I try to keep Freddie on the path, close to me, but of course he soon starts to veer away.

"Can I go on the slide for a bit?" Freddie asks, pulling at me.

"No, not yet," I tell him. "We'll be late for Nan and Grandad."

I know they will worry if we are late.

Freddie starts dragging his feet along the ground. He has that annoying pouty look on his face. "We never go to the playground any more," he moans. "Mum never takes me."

I sigh. I feel bad because it's true. We don't go any more. It's something Steve always used to do with us, taking us all to the park for an hour or so. Then he'd insist we play some football on the field – even though Mum and I were rubbish and kept falling over. We'd end up sitting together on the field, puffed out and enjoying ice creams that Steve had bought from the van in the car park. How have things changed so quickly?

"Maybe we can pop in on the way back," I say.

"Really?" Freddie replies.

"Yeah. I'm sure Mum won't mind if we're home a bit later."

Besides, it will give her even more time to rest.

Nan and Grandad live on the main street that leads into town. Their house is a grand Victorian detached building that backs onto the railway. Both Freddie and I love it. Freddie does because he can watch the trains rumbling past from the large back garden. I do because it looks a bit like a house of horrors, with its shuttered, arched windows and detailed corner turrets.

Nan already has the kettle on when we arrive. I can hear it whistling as soon as she opens the front door to us. Freddie steams into the kitchen, searching for the nice biscuits that Nan always lays out. He finds Grandad there waiting for him, already unwrapping Freddie's favourite chocolate ones.

"Don't eat too many," I call after him. "Or you'll be sick."

Nan laughs. "You really look after him, don't you?" Then her eyes scan behind me and a tiny frown creases across her forehead. "Where's your mum?" Nan asks. "Isn't she coming?"

I slip off my coat and place my shoes on the mat like always. "No, Nan. She says she is too tired today."

"Really?" Nan says, and shakes her head softly. "Did she go back to bed then?"

"She's just resting on the sofa. Watching TV."

"I see."

Nan follows me into the kitchen and starts to fuss around, making us some drinks. Freddie is talking with his mouth full. I shake my head at him and frown.

"He's excited," Grandad explains. "I found this in the loft. It used to be your mum's. I'm surprised it's lasted as well as it has."

I peer down at the table in front of them. It's some kind of wooden frame with bright blue material attached. I frown, unsure.

"I need to fix it," Grandad says.

"It's a kite!" says Freddie, spraying crumbs everywhere.

"Oh." I reach forward and stroke the thin fabric. It is so soft and delicate. "This really used to be Mum's?" I ask.

"Oh yes!" Grandad holds the kite up properly so I can see its shape better. It is torn down one side and part of the frame has snapped, but I can make it out much clearer now. "Your mum absolutely loved it," Grandad says. "We used to go up to Gorse Hill and fly it for hours. She never got bored."

"How old was she then?"

"Oh – let's see. About your age – thirteen, fourteen."

I look at Grandad, amazed. It is hard enough picturing Mum as a young girl but even harder picturing her doing something like this. Obviously I have seen photos of her. She looked like a skinnier version of me. But I'd never really thought about what she might have been into. Of all things, I wouldn't have guessed kite flying.

"Grandad is going to fix it so we can fly it too," Freddie says, his eyes sparkling. "Won't that be cool?"

"Yes," I say. "That really will be."

*

Nan stops me in the hall before we leave that evening. Freddie is still in the living room saying goodbye to Grandad – as usual he is taking ages.

"Is everything OK, Violet?" Nan asks softly. Her hand skates across my back, like she wants to give me a squeeze but has thought better of it.

"I'm just fed up with Freddie taking for ever to get ready," I say, and glance at the clock. "We can't be too late back. Mum will worry."

Or would she. Really? I wonder.

"I can always call her," Nan suggests. "Tell her you're on your way?"

"It's OK," I say. "I can do that."

"Then why are you worried?"

I shrug. "I dunno ..."

Because, Nan, there is a chance that Mum isn't just resting on the sofa. There is a chance that she has got herself some more drink from somewhere. If that's the case, she won't be answering any calls from me.

44

There's also a chance that the mum we go home to will be angry. Or loud. Or tearful.

And so there's a big part of me that doesn't want to go home at all ...

"You would tell me, Violet. You would tell me if anything else was going on," Nan says firmly. "If you're worried about your mum at all. If you think—"

I move away from Nan, hold up my hands. "Nan. Mum is fine. Honestly."

The lies slip easily from my lips.

Nan slowly nods. "Fair enough," she says. "But if you ever are worried, you tell us. OK?"

"OK," I whisper.

But how can I?

If I tell Nan how bad Mum is getting, Mum will never, ever forgive me. I'd be breaking her trust.

And how can I give Nan even more things to worry about? Doesn't she have enough to deal with, looking after Grandad?

I have to believe that this is still just a blip.

I have to believe it will all be over soon.

*

When we walk into the house, Mum is asleep on the sofa, still wearing her pyjamas. The TV is still blaring an annoying show. Beside her is a glass of water.

Relief floods me. She hasn't moved.

I guide Freddie into the kitchen, my finger on my lips. I can make his tea. I will make sure everything is nice and clean for when Mum wakes up again.

Let Mum rest ... She needs it.

It is only when I open the bin to throw away Freddie's toast crusts that I see it.

An empty vodka bottle.

And it wasn't there before.

FIVE

When the school bell rings at the end of the day on Monday, my body sags with relief. I struggle most Mondays as it is, but this one has been particularly difficult.

At least Mum was up and awake this morning. At least she took Freddie to school. The last thing I need is another late mark and a stupid detention.

"You look exhausted," Ness says as we gather our stuff together. "Are you sure you still want to come to the shops with me?"

"I'm fine," I reply, slinging my bag on my back. "Just a bit tired, that's all. I could do with some fresh air."

It is a hot, sticky afternoon, so the lessons have been particularly painful. I am already craving a cool ice cream and a drink. I picture me and Ness sitting in the park and chilling. Maybe I can talk to her about what is going on ...

We file out down the corridor, fighting against the crowds.

"Dan might be at the shops," Ness whispers, her cheeks turning pink. "At least I think he might. His mum normally picks him up from the shops."

I nudge her. "I knew there must be another reason you're so keen to go."

"What?" Ness says, and holds up her hands innocently. "He's just nice to look at, that's all."

We both giggle. Ness has been in love with Dan since primary school. It is just a shame he doesn't seem to notice that she exists.

We carry on chatting as we move out of the building and I nearly miss it. It is so noisy all around me, I almost don't hear my own phone. It's Ness who turns to me, her nose wrinkled.

"Isn't that yours?" Ness asks.

I pull my mobile out, confused for a second as I normally put it on silent in the mornings ready for when I am in school. I must have forgotten today in the rush to get out. That's what oversleeping does to you. It makes you forget stuff.

I don't recognise the number calling me. I see that I have already missed two calls from them. An icy feeling swells in my stomach. This can't be good. But I have to answer it.

Tentatively I swipe the phone. "Hello?" I say.

"Hello. Is that Violet, Freddie's sister?" The voice on the other end is polite but also sounds concerned. "This is Freddie's teacher, Mrs Wilson."

I know Mrs Wilson from when I drop Freddie off. She is a nice, kind lady who always takes Freddie's hand when he is scared.

"Yes, it is. Is he OK?" I reply, panic building.

"Oh, he's fine. He's fine," Mrs Wilson says softly. "It's just ... well, your mum hasn't come to collect him yet. Freddie's still here waiting. I wondered if there was a problem. I can't get hold of her, you see ..."

My eyes scan the clock on the school wall. It is nearly half past three now. Freddie finished at three o'clock. Where the hell is Mum?

"Oh ... Oh, I'm so sorry," I say quickly. "I can come and get him right away. Is he OK?"

"He's fine," Mrs Wilson says. "A bit upset, but I've got him doing some colouring now." She pauses. "But, Violet, I need to know where your mum is. We're concerned—"

"Mum is fine," I interrupt. "She must have forgotten to tell you that she has an appointment this afternoon, with the doctor." The excuses are coming at speed. "This is all my fault. I totally forgot to leave school early. Tell Freddie I'm sorry and I'll be there as soon as I can ..."

"But, Violet—"

"Please, Mrs Wilson, just tell Freddie that. This is all my fault. I feel awful."

I shut off the call, tears blinding my eyes. Ness looks at me, horrified. She circles in front of me.

"What's going on, Vee?" Ness asked. "What's happened?"

"Nothing. Nothing is going on," I bite back. "I just need to sort something out."

Then I rush off, leaving Ness staring after me, probably wondering why on earth I suddenly snapped at her like that.

Freddie is sitting at the back of the classroom when I run in. He still has his coat on and his cheeks are all puffy and red. I know right away that he has been crying. Mrs Wilson is sitting next to him. She jumps up as soon as I walk in and flashes me a tired smile.

"Vee," Freddie says, looking up as I approach. "Where were you? I thought you weren't going to come. Where's Mum?" His questions tumble out too fast.

"Mum has an appointment, remember?" I stare at Freddie hard, willing him to understand. "It's my fault. I forgot! You know how silly my brain is sometimes."

Freddie frowns. "But you never forget anything."

"That's not true," I reply. Even though we both know it is. It isn't me that has difficulty remembering stuff.

I even checked with Mum this morning. I grabbed her arm before I left the house and reminded her that she had to collect Freddie. Like always. She just nodded back at me, like I was over-reacting. "Of course I'll be there," she said. "Where else would I be?"

Where else indeed? I don't know – she's not answering her phone.

Mrs Wilson gestures for me to walk over to her desk with her. I can tell she is uneasy. Her body is all stiff and awkward.

"Violet, I will need to talk to the Head about this. I'm a bit concerned."

"There's no need to be. It's just a mistake," I say, my frustration growing. "It's no big deal."

"I just need to log it, that's all," Mrs Wilson tells me. "When a parent doesn't collect—"

I hold up my hand to stop her. "My mum will speak to you tomorrow, OK? She'll explain everything." I point at Freddie, who is folding up his drawing. "Look – he's fine now," I say. "He's absolutely fine. There's really nothing to worry about."

Mrs Wilson nods slowly. "OK, but I'll need to speak to your mum tomorrow morning."

"Of course," I reply.

I walk back over and take Freddie's clammy hand in mine. I flash him my brightest smile. It hurts my cheeks.

"Come on, let's go home," I tell him. "I bet Mummy is there waiting for us now."

I know Mum is home as soon as I see her car on the drive. My skin bristles. If she is here, why on earth didn't she pick up Freddie?

You know the answer ... I tell myself. *You know why she didn't show up.*

You always knew why ...

My throat is so dry it feels like it is coated with dust. I squeeze Freddie's hand and ease him behind me as I open the door. I call out for Mum, but there is no reply.

"Is she here?" Freddie asks. "Where is she?"

"Wait here, Freddie," I say softly. "I just want to see where Mum is."

Freddie kicks off his shoes and scowls. "I want to watch the telly."

"And you can in a minute. Just hang on."

The radio is blaring from the kitchen with a discussion programme. Some guy is chattering on about his favourite holiday destination and a woman is laughing loudly. Their voices seem eerily out of place in the hollow house.

"... I just love the feel of the sun on my face when I go away, don't you?"

"As long as I can relax with a cold glass of wine, I don't care ..."

I walk briskly into the living room. It is empty, but I notice that both Mum's phones are on the coffee table, next to a full cup of black coffee.

"Mum ..." I say again, the blood racing through my veins.

The radio is on too loud. The voices are annoying me with their bright, over-the-top chatter.

"It's all about family, isn't it? Spending time with the people you love ..."

I stride into the kitchen towards our smart speaker and order it to shut up. The sudden silence is deafening.

"Mum?" I repeat.

The kitchen is a complete mess. Mum hasn't bothered putting the breakfast stuff in the dishwasher and everything is still out on the breakfast bar. Freddie's bowl of Coco Pops is congealing in the late-afternoon sun. His spilt chocolate milk is still a dark puddle on the countertop.

And there is a bottle sitting on the side. A large empty bottle of vodka.

I turn towards the conservatory, towards Mum's workspace. I guess I am still expecting to see her there, her nose stuck in a magazine, waiting for her next client.

What I do see takes the breath right out of my lungs.

"Mum!" I shout.

She is there all right. But not sitting on the chair as I hoped. Instead she is sprawled on the tiled floor, with broken glass gleaming all around her.

And she isn't moving.

SIX

For a moment I am frozen, rooted to the spot. My eyes are fixed on Mum's bent body. A million thoughts flood my mind all at once:

Oh my god, she's dead.

I can't deal with this. I can't do this.

Mum …

Is she actually dead?

What the hell do I do?

And then Freddie calls me. His bright, slightly scared voice wakes me up from my short paralysis.

"Vee – can I come in yet?" Freddie says.

"Just – just wait there, Fred!" I shout back.

He can't see this. He would be so frightened. I have to sort it out.

Running over to Mum, I call out to her again, softly. My feet crunch on the broken glass and I am so thankful that I haven't yet taken my shoes off.

"What's going on?" Freddie yells.

"There's broken glass out here," I tell him. "I don't want you cutting yourself."

I bend down towards Mum. I push aside the hair that has fallen across her face. Her mouth is open slightly and her skin has a sweaty sheen to it. "Mum!" I say again.

Mum groans softly. Her eyes gently flicker and then open. "Vee ..."

Her breath is sour. I back away a little.

"Mum," I say. "What's happened ...?"

"I ..." she starts to reply. She is slurring. She moves her head and groans again, her eyes blinking against the light. "Where am I?"

"In the conservatory," I say. "I think you fell." I peer down at Mum's hand, which I can now see is bleeding. "You must've been holding a glass at the time. You've cut yourself."

Mum slowly pulls herself up into a sitting position, groaning all the time and rubbing the back of her head with her non-cut hand.

"Have you hurt your head?" I ask. "We need to check that ..."

"It's ... It's fine ..." Mum shivers and looks down at her hand like she hasn't seen it before. "I don't ... I don't remember."

Mum's words sound too fat for her mouth. She looks at me and smiles. It's a flimsy smile. A smile that she always seems to put on when she has been drinking. Her red-rimmed eyes are watering.

"My hand—" She holds it out for me to see.

The cut looks deep. "You might need stitches," I say, then pause. "Mum, we need to get you to hospital. We need to make sure you're OK."

"No!" Mum begins to pull herself up, using a chair for support. Her legs are buckling under her weight. She has to take a moment or two to steady herself and then breathes out hard. "See! I'm fine!" She giggles.

"But your hand isn't and your head needs to be looked at," I tell her.

I remember when Freddie fell on the playground last year. Mum had been so worried because he'd hit his head on the concrete. "He might have concussion," she'd said, insisting that he be checked over at hospital. "You have to be careful with things like that."

But this version of Mum is so different. She is looking at me with shiny eyes and a gaping mouth. The acrid smell of alcohol is all over her. I can still smell it even as I step away.

She must've been drinking all day.

"Pass me …" she starts, and points a wobbly finger at a nearby dish cloth. I give it to her and watch as she clumsily ties it around her hand. Then she nods, satisfied, and flops down heavily on the chair.

"What happened, Mum?" I whisper.

I see that her eyes are woozy. Her head is lolling on her neck, barely able to stay still.

"I fell …" Mum shrugs. "That's all."

"But, Mum …"

"Shhh!" She holds up her uninjured hand to her mouth. "Shhh. Not now."

Her eyes slowly close and I watch as she slips into another drunken sleep.

I call Nan. I really don't want to bother her, but what other choice do I have? Mum is now fast asleep on the chair, snoring softly. Freddie is sitting quietly at the breakfast bar, eating a cheese sandwich I made for him. But he is really only nibbling on it. His eyes keep drifting over to Mum. I have tried to reassure him she's OK, but I don't think it has worked very well. Freddie isn't stupid.

Nan arrives just as I have finished sweeping the floor and mopping up Mum's blood. She runs into the kitchen and eyes up the scene. Nan sees Mum and groans softly. Her shoulders sag and she slowly shakes her head.

"What happened?" Nan asks me.

"I don't know." I go to throw away the last of the bloody kitchen towel and gesture inside the bin. "I found this when I came home."

Nan looks and sees the empty bottle of vodka nestled there. Her hand touches my back. "I see ..."

"I don't know what to do," I whisper. "Mum didn't collect Freddie from school and then I came home ..."

I realise that shaky sobs are taking over my body. Nan pulls me towards her and I fold up into her arms.

"I'm sorry," Nan whispers. "I didn't realise how bad things were getting. I've been so distracted with your grandad."

"It's not your fault ..." I mumble into her arm.

"It'll be OK," Nan soothes. "I'll stay over tonight. I'll talk to your mum in the morning."

"But what about Grandad?" I ask.

"Grandad will be fine for one night," she says smoothly. "Right now I need to focus on you three."

I sink back into her arms. Right now that is all I need to hear.

*

Later, in bed, I can hear the gentle murmur of the TV downstairs. I know Nan is there, watching her soaps and sipping her tea. A gentle feeling of reassurance washes over me. Freddie is already asleep. Nan bathed him and read him a bedtime story. Then she managed to wake Mum up and help her upstairs. In the space of a few hours, Nan has tidied up the whole mess of our house and tucked us all safely away again.

I am so grateful to her.

But as I stare at my closed door, another feeling sweeps over me. A grumbling fear that is so deep and so strong it is difficult to ignore.

Nan shouldn't be here. She should be in her own house. With Grandad.

She should be keeping him safe.

We were so lucky before, when Grandad had a heart attack. He was taken to hospital just in time. They managed to save him. Now Grandad has a pacemaker in his chest to regulate his heartbeats. But even so, it was all so worrying. We nearly lost him.

The last thing I want is for him to be on his own. Grandad needs Nan. What if something happens again and he is by himself? Nan should be with him, not worrying about us. This is all wrong.

None of this is fair.

I grip my duvet and stare at the wall that stands between me and Mum. I imagine her spread out on her bed, her hair a mess, her breath stinking, her make-up all smudged across her face.

And for the first time in my life, a part of me actually hates her.

SEVEN

A fresh start. This time Mum swears it will be different.

"I won't drink any more," Mum says firmly the next morning. We are all sitting together after breakfast and Mum is still in her pyjamas. Mum has phoned the school and told them I won't be in today. She lied and said I have a tummy ache. This isn't too far from the truth, as my tummy does feel sore and swollen. There is no way I can face school today, especially as I've hardly slept. Nan has already taken Freddie to his school and has been to check in on Grandad, and now she is back with us. She looks as tired as I do, although she'll never admit to it.

"You promise?" I ask Mum.

"I just had a wobble. That's all. I'm going to be different now. I'm going to be how I used to be."

There. Mum has made a promise. Her face is pale, stripped bare of its usual colour, and under her eyes are smudges of dark shadows.

I stare at her, disbelieving. A wobble? Is that all it was? My focus is fixed on her skinny white hands and how she can't seem to keep them still.

Nan hugs Mum and kisses her softly on the head. "That's such a relief to hear," Nan says. "But you've been through so much. Maybe you should get some professional help?"

Mum flinches at the suggestion.

"No. No. I'm fine. It's not that bad." Mum smiles. It is her steady reassuring smile. It always worked well in the past. It brightens her entire face. I can see Nan relax a little.

"And you won't forget to pick up Freddie again?" I say.

"No. Of course not," Mum replies, and stares at me as if I am crazy. "I will never do that again. That was one mistake. I'll speak to his teacher about that today and explain."

Nan squeezes her hand and says, "You can always come and stay with us? We have the room?"

"No." Mum's reply is firm. "Thank you, but no. I need to get my life back on track again and that means meeting my clients and cutting some hair. I don't want to move out of my house and I don't want to unsettle the kids any more."

Nan nods. "Perhaps I can go back home then," she says, "if you're sure …" Her forehead creases with concern.

"Of course you should go back. Dad needs you," Mum says softly. "It was so good of you to stay over, but I've got to get my routine back. It'll help me."

"If you're sure?" Nan asks. I can tell she is still worried.

"I'm sure."

But that doesn't stop Nan taking me to one side before she leaves. "If you're worried about anything, just call me," she says. "I'll come over straight away."

"OK," I reply.

"Do you promise?"

"I promise."

I count the days as they pass and everything seems to be going as it should be. I try to let myself relax. I try to tell myself that everything is fine.

Day one

Mum gets out of bed on time. She makes me and Freddie breakfast. She sits quietly at the table and listens as Freddie talks excitedly. Mum isn't smiling much, but she is there with us. She takes Freddie to school and kisses my cheek at the door before I leave. Her breath smells fresh, of mint.

I get through my own day. I manage to concentrate in Maths. I walk home with Ness and she squeezes my hand and tells me that I look tired.

The truth is that I am tired. But I just smile and reply that everything is fine.

Day three

Mum is up before me. She has already cleaned the kitchen and is drinking coffee at the table. She asks me what I would like for dinner later. She tells me she is going to go shopping to get some "nice food in". She is making a list.

At school I try not to panic as I imagine Mum walking past the drink aisle in the supermarket. I picture all those shelves of temptation. My English teacher, Mrs Humphries, shouts at me for "daydreaming" and I cringe as the whole class turn to stare at me.

I go home with a headache, but dinner is waiting as promised. And Mum is smiling and seems relaxed. She hardly eats anything herself though.

Day four

Mum actually has a decent phone call with Steve without shouting at him. She tells Freddie that his dad is going to come and visit soon. I see the brief look of pain on her face as Freddie yells with delight – "Yeah! Daddy!" But Mum doesn't get angry, she just nods and leaves the room.

Ness messages me, asking how I am – and once again I tell her that everything is fine. Because it is, isn't it? I tell Ness that Mum has just been ill with flu and that we are getting back on track. No one knows that I am still checking the cupboards to make sure there are no hidden bottles anywhere. No one knows that I can't stop staring at Mum – watching her drink her bottled water, hoping it is a good sign that her hands are no longer shaking.

So far, so good.

I try to relax. I try to believe.

By day eleven, Mum has decided that it is time for us to do something nice together as a family. She suggests the cinema and I agree. It has been so long since we have done anything like that. Freddie really wants to see the new Lego movie, so we book three tickets. It feels like we are actually going to have a decent weekend again.

Mum is looking good. She has spent time in the bathroom getting ready and has drenched herself in perfume. In fact, it is a bit too strong and makes me cough.

"Sorry!" Mum says, blushing. "I just want to feel good."

"You look lovely," I say, gazing at her carefully made-up face. She has pulled her hair up into a bun and it makes her look really sophisticated.

Mum giggles and replies, "You look lovely too."

That is hardly true. I am just dressed in my jeans and baggy top and have simply dragged a brush through my unruly hair. But I don't care. Mum is more bothered about these things than me. The fact that she is making an effort again just proves that she is getting better.

Mum drives us into town and parks right outside the multiplex cinema. For a moment she sits in the car, gripping the wheel and taking some long, shaky breaths.

"Are you OK?" I ask, worried.

Mum nods slowly. "Just felt a bit shaky there for a moment. I'll be fine. You must stop worrying about me."

We load up with popcorn and drinks and sit ourselves in the best seats, right in the centre.

Freddie is sitting between us on a wobbly booster seat. He is so excited he can barely sit still. I am scared he is going to wobble himself off.

"This is the best day," Freddie says, and plunges his hand into the popcorn. "I love it here. Can we stay for ever?"

Mum just smiles at him.

I settle back as the film starts and try to lose myself in the loud noises and bright action characters. It is nice to be somewhere else for a change – in another world not at all like my own. Even Freddie is still, his face transfixed as he watches the screen.

I lean over to look at Mum. I am going to whisper something about Freddie's face and how cute he looks. But then I see that her eyes are closed and her mouth is slightly open. Despite the noise inside the cinema, Mum is fast asleep.

I turn back to the film and try to get back into the action, but it is hard to ignore the heavy knot that has returned to my stomach. Why is Mum so tired?

Mum takes us to McDonald's after. We manage to get a table at the back and hungrily eat our burgers and fries. Well, Freddie and I do. Mum has a coffee and a chicken wrap, but she barely touches it.

"Aren't you hungry?" I ask her.

"Not really." Mum sips her coffee. "I ate earlier."

I'm pretty sure this isn't true. I can't remember Mum eating before we went out – I just recall her guzzling bottled water a few hours ago.

"You should eat," I say, pointing at her wrap.

Mum always loved eating before. When Steve lived with us, she cooked huge elaborate meals. She used to fill her plate and giggle about the amount of calories she was "putting away".

"You sound like your nan again," Mum says, and sighs. She lifts the wrap to her mouth, then nibbles at it half-heartedly. "My stomach has shrunk a bit. That's all. I never feel up to eating much."

"How can your stomach shrink?" Freddie asks as he looks up, alarmed. "Will that happen to me?"

"That'll never happen to you, baby." Mum ruffles his hair and chuckles as he takes another mouthful of his burger. "See! You eat so well. You're growing fast."

"I'm going to be tall like Daddy," Freddie says.

Mum pauses and then replies, "Yes. Yes, you will. And handsome too."

I see something pass across Mum's face. A shadow of sadness.

"You still miss him, don't you?" I say.

Mum looks at me. Her eyes hold my gaze. They are clearer today, almost icy blue in colour. She blinks and I can see the layer of tears in her eyes.

"I miss him," Freddie says instead. "I miss him a lot."

Mum pulls him towards her. "We all do," she whispers. "We all do."

It is the first time I have realised how sad she really is.

EIGHT

"I'm so sorry," Mum says after I finish my breakfast on Monday morning. She looks at me with a worried stare. "I was hoping I wouldn't have to ask you so soon, but I need to make up for the appointments I missed. Mrs Winters can only come here at eight-thirty this morning. Can you take Freddie to school?"

"It's fine," I tell her. "It's only a one-off."

I know Mum can't help it when it comes to work and it is important that she keeps busy. As she keeps on saying – we need to get back on track.

"Thank you." Mum pulls me into a hug. "I'd ask your nan, but she has to take Grandad to his doctor's appointment this morning."

"It's OK," I say. "I just hope Freddie can cope with the bus."

And I can get into school without getting a late code ...

Mum smiles. "I'm just going to jump in the shower then. Get myself ready. Freddie's lunch is in the fridge – don't forget it."

I nod and watch as Mum swirls out of the kitchen, leaving behind her strong perfume scent.

Freddie is finishing his cereal at the table. He looks up at me, a milky moustache above his upper lip.

"Why isn't Mum taking me to school?" he asks.

"Because she really needs to work." I pause, then add, "But it'll be OK. If we leave early, we can be at the front of the queue at the bus stop. Maybe that way we can make sure we get a seat."

Freddie nods. "That'll be better."

"Well, hurry up and wash your face and we can go," I tell him.

I move around the kitchen quickly, loading up the dishwasher and cleaning the worktop. Then I send Ness a message:

I might be late. Please don't wait for me.

I find Freddie's lunch nestled at the back of the fridge, all packed and ready. Freddie hates school dinners. He says they make him sick.

"I'm ready!" he shouts from the hall.

I find Freddie tugging on his coat. He's already put his shoes on – for once he seems keen to leave. I guess the idea of getting to the front of the bus queue has worked. It is only as we are leaving the house that Freddie notices his bag is missing something.

"My water bottle," he says. "I haven't got my water bottle!"

I'm not sure where it is – it wasn't with his lunch. I go to call for Mum, but I can already hear the hiss of the shower – she will never hear me over that.

"I need to take my drink." Freddie pouts. "The water at school tastes nasty."

I go back in the kitchen to see if it is there, but I can't find it. I open the fridge again and see Mum's water bottles all lined up in a row, ready to go.

Surely she wouldn't miss one?

I don't really have time to think about it, so I grab the nearest bottle and run back to the front door.

"All sorted, Freddie," I say, squeezing the lovely cool bottle into his bag. "All sorted."

Ness is waiting for me at the school gates. She smiles nervously as soon as she sees me and grabs my arm.

"Come on, we'll be late," Ness says.

"I told you not to wait for me," I reply.

Ness shrugs. "It's not a problem. Besides, the bell has only just gone. We might be OK."

I don't bother to tell Ness what a rush it has been. I only had time to leave Freddie in the playground before rushing up the hill to school. I am just praying he is OK. Freddie always looks so small and nervous when I leave him on his own.

"How come you had to take Freddie again?" Ness asks.

"My mum has to cut hair early this morning." I smile at her. "She's really busy today."

Ness smiles back at me. "So – that's good then? Is your mum better now? You can finally start to chill out a bit?"

"I guess," I reply, feeling tense.

We walk up the main steps towards the school building. People are still running inside and there are no signs of any teachers yet. I breathe out. Hopefully we are going to make it this time with no detention.

Ness nudges me as we slip inside. "Maybe we can start doing stuff again," she says. "You know, like hanging out after school?"

Guilt prickles at me. I can't remember when I last spent any real time with Ness. I've always been in such a rush to get home to Mum.

"Yeah. That'll be nice," I say.

We walk into tutor group giggling softly as Ness whispers the latest gossip to me. I drift into the room and feel like a weight is shifting off my shoulders.

Today really is going to be a good day.

Except it isn't. It *really* isn't.

How could I have been so dumb to think it would be?

I know something is wrong as soon as I see Mr Deacon, the Deputy Head, walk into my English lesson. It is one of those really quiet lessons where everyone is actually working pretty hard, but even the lowest murmurs stop as soon as he strides in. His eyes scan the room and soon fall on me. I've never been in serious trouble before, but right away I begin sweating like crazy. Mr Deacon only comes into class if you have done something badly wrong. Is this about earlier? Was I caught sneaking in late again? Have I done it one too many times?

Ness nudges me, asking, "What's he here for?"

Mr Deacon is whispering something to our English teacher, Mrs Humphries. They both look up at me.

"Violet, can I borrow you for a moment?" Mr Deacon asks.

"Yeah, sure," I croak, putting down my pen.

I stand up. My legs are wobbling. I can feel the eyes of the entire class on me.

"You'd better bring your bag as well," Mr Deacon says.

I pick it up, shoving my books inside. My stomach is doing a loop-the-loop. This has to be bad. If he is telling me to take all my stuff, it has to be a big deal.

Unless it is Mum …

The thought hits me like a stinging slap. Has Mum fallen again? Is she seriously hurt this time? I feel suddenly giddy and have to grip the side of the desk to support myself.

"It'll be all right," Ness whispers. But even she sounds unsure.

I pick up my bag and unsteadily follow Mr Deacon out of the class, hoping desperately that I'm not about to vomit in front of everyone.

Mr Deacon takes me straight to the Head Teacher's office. I've only ever been there once and that was to pick up an award. I am never normally in trouble. This isn't me. Even standing outside the wood-panelled door sends me into a panic.

"Am I in trouble?" I gasp at Mr Deacon. "Is it my mum? Is she OK?"

Mr Deacon peers over at me from behind his thick glasses. He seems sad, not angry. "Your mum is fine, Violet, as far as I'm aware," Mr Deacon says. "But there is someone here who needs to speak to you."

He pushes open the door and, feeling confused, I follow him in.

Our Head Teacher, Mr Yeats, is sitting at the small round table at the side of his office. Next to him are a lady and a man that I don't recognise. They have lanyards around their necks and the woman has a notepad in front of her.

Mr Yeats thanks Mr Deacon and gestures for me to come over. He waits for the door to close and then asks me to sit down.

"I'm sorry to pull you out of a lesson, Violet," Mr Yeats says, "but we need to speak to you about something. Something very important."

I nod numbly. *OK. What?*

The woman smiles at me. She is young and pretty with long blonde hair and bright highlights. Mum would have commented on how nice they look.

"Violet, my name is Amy Winters," she says. "And this is Ben Denton. We are social workers."

I stare hard at them, these two smiley people. I know about social workers. I've heard things muttered about them in school. I remember when Ness told me about Seb Roberts in our class – he had been taken away from his parents by people like this. They come to break families up. They ruin lives.

"You're not in trouble, Violet," Ben says. "We're here to help." He has longish dark hair that flops in front of his eyes. When he smiles, I notice that his teeth are slightly crooked.

"I don't want to talk to social workers," I say, and turn to Mr Yeats. "Please, can I just go back to class? I don't want to be here."

Mr Yeats smiles softly. I've always liked him. He isn't one of those shouty teachers – he seems to be someone who always has time to listen. His eyes glisten and he leans forward a little. "Violet – as Mr Denton says, you are not in trouble," Mr Yeats says. "They are just here to ask some questions. That's all. We just need you to be as honest as possible."

Honest? I blink and then shrug.

"OK ..." I say.

"Violet," Amy Winters begins. Her voice is gentle but firm. "You took your younger brother to school this morning, didn't you?"

I nod slowly. "Yes. Why?" I pause. "Is this all because I was late again? Because I promise—"

Amy holds out her hand. "No, Violet," she says, "it's not that. But why did you take Freddie to school?"

"Because Mum had a client coming to the house. She's a hairdresser," I explain. I am talking too fast, I know it. "Mum normally doesn't book early appointments, but she'd already cancelled this one once ..."

Amy smiles at me. "That's OK, Violet. I understand."

"So, *I* don't understand what the problem is?" I say.

"Violet – who made Freddie's packed lunch and drink?" Ben asks this time.

I frown. "Mum makes his lunch. She always does. I just grabbed it from the fridge."

"And his drink?" Ben goes on. "Your mum made that too?"

I shake my head, confused. "Well, no. I couldn't find his normal bottle, so I took one of Mum's bottled waters that were already made up. She won't mind. I can't see why that's a problem."

They are all looking at me. Amy is chewing her lip. Ben is scribbling something on his notepad. Finally, he speaks again.

"You see, Violet, that's the problem. It wasn't water in that bottle. It was vodka. Neat vodka. And Freddie drank some at school this morning."

NINE

The room is spinning around and around. I think people are talking to me, but I can't hear them properly.

Freddie. Freddie has drunk neat vodka.

How ...

How has this happened?

"Violet?" someone says. I'm not even sure who.

The water ... It was bottled water. Mum is always drinking it.

It is just water.

Mum ...

My head snaps up. "Is he OK?" I ask. "Freddie. Is he going to be OK?"

"Freddie is fine," Amy says. She leans across the table to look at me and gently taps my hand. "He took a gulp and it made him cough and he got a little bit upset. Of course his teacher then noticed that Freddie was distressed and took the bottle from him."

"But he'll be OK?" I say.

"Yes, he'll be fine."

"But the question is, how did he end up with that drink in his bag?" Ben says quietly. He has stopped writing and is staring right at me, his eyebrow raised slightly. "You're not in any trouble, Violet. We just need to know how an alcoholic drink ended up in a water bottle like that."

"I ..." I start, and shift on my seat, feeling sweat curling down my neck. "I'm not sure—"

"We will be talking to your mum of course, as well," Amy says. She pauses before adding, "It's not just this incident that worries us, Violet. Both your school and Freddie's have mentioned your attendance. You have been late a few times.

87

Mr Yeats has concerns about you. He says that you have been struggling in school recently. Teachers have noticed that you seem tired and unable to focus, and your usual high standard of work is dropping."

"I'm fine," I say, and shake my head again. "I have trouble sleeping. That's all."

"But is that all?" Mr Yeats asks gently. "We are aware that you seem to be doing a lot more at home. Your mum hasn't been very good at returning our calls lately to address our concerns. That's not like her at all." Mr Yeats turns to the social workers. "We are certainly of the view that things have slipped in the last year or so."

"Nothing has slipped," I snap. "Mum just has a lot of work to do and I try to help where I can. It's not too much for me."

"But this morning?" Ben asks.

"This morning was my mistake," I reply quickly. "Mine. Mum had told me that she had some drink left over. She ... She said she had put it in a smaller bottle to store it. I just forgot. I was in a rush and I grabbed the nearest one without checking."

Ben scribbles something else on his pad.

"Are you sure that's what happened?" Amy asks.

"Of course I'm sure," I say. "My mum is allowed to have a drink now and again, isn't she? She told me about the bottle. This is all my fault. I was rushing."

Amy and Ben both look at me. Then Ben slowly nods and puts his pen down.

"I'm sorry," I say softly. "I really am. But you don't need to bother my mum about this now, do you?"

Ben looks at me with what seems like a sad expression. "Oh yes," he says. "We still need to speak to your mum."

I grip the side of my chair and wonder if the shaky feeling will ever go away.

If they speak to my mum, what on earth will she say?

Will she ever forgive me?

The bell rings for lunch and they say I can go. But first Amy takes me to one side and tells me that I should speak to someone if I have "any other concerns".

I tell her I am fine. I don't know how many times I have had to say this recently. I wonder if I should stamp it on my head.

I'm OK. Everything is fine.

Just leave me alone.

Mr Yeats pats my arm as I leave the room.

"Don't feel bad," he says. "It was an easy mistake to make."

I am confused at first, wondering what he means. Then I realise that he is talking about the bottle and the lie I have just told. My cheeks burn red and I stammer out a quick "thank you" before scuttling away.

I can't face the lunch hall. I'm not hungry at all – my stomach has shrunk to half its size and my throat feels closed up and tight. I can't face all the people either. Even the thought of sitting with Ness and her asking me what is going on makes me feel sick. What can I tell her?

Oh, my mum told me that she had given up drinking. And do you know what? I believed her.

What sort of idiot am I? I watched Mum guzzling her stupid water and felt so pleased and proud of her for being healthy, when all the time she has been drinking neat vodka. Why did I never think to check it? Why didn't I sniff it?

And because of that, because I was so stupid to believe Mum, I gave my four-year-old brother one of her "special drinks" to take to school.

That's the kind of idiot I am.

I walk into the nearest girls' toilets and shut myself away in a cubicle. I'm trying not cry, but it is hard not to.

How stupid am I? Why didn't I notice?

I know why. Because I can hardly remember what Mum looks like when she hasn't had a drink, that's why. Because this has become the new normal for us. OK, so Mum might not have been off her face the last few weeks, but she has still been drinking regularly – topping herself up with her "water".

When was Mum last sober? Properly sober ...? I have no idea.

I'm not sure I know who my mum is any more.

Blindly, I reach for my mobile. There is a message from Ness, but I ignore it. I'll face her later, when I feel ready.

My finger hovers over Mum's number.

I could call her. I could warn her about what has just happened. I could tell her what I have said so that our stories match. I could stop her getting into trouble.

I keep staring at the phone screen, my mouth dry, my eyes wet with tears.

But I can't do it. I can't bring myself to speak to her.

So instead I scroll down. I press another name. I listen patiently as the dial tone rings. When they finally answer, I attempt to speak.

"Hello—" I begin.

But the tears take over.

TEN

It is so quiet at Nan and Grandad's house, I feel like I could curl up on the sofa and sleep for ever. Well, I could if my mind would let me. As usual it is racing – too full of thoughts and worries. My stomach is like a squashed-up ball inside me that hurts so much when I move.

All I can do is sit and try to concentrate on my breathing. I don't want to cry. Not again. I've already done too much of that.

Freddie is stretched out on the floor beside me, colouring in one of his books. He really doesn't seem to have a clue what is going on. To him, it is just a nice treat being here. To Freddie, none of this is a big deal. But I know different. Nan brought us back here after I called her. I don't really know what is happening, but I do know that the social workers were speaking to Mum this afternoon. When she came back to Nan's house, she looked completely wiped out. I have been shooed out of the kitchen, where my grandparents and Mum are talking quietly now. But I saw their serious faces. Mum has hardly been able to look at me. Does she blame me for all of this?

All I can do now is sit here and wait.

"Are we staying here tonight?" Freddie asks suddenly.

"I don't know," I say, clenching my fists. "I think so."

"Why?"

"Just ... just because ..."

"Is Mum staying as well?"

"I don't know," I tell him.

"I think she should," Freddie says softly, still scribbling. "I think Mum should stay here with us."

I blink, trying to force away the tears. "Maybe ... I don't know, Freddie."

I can't tell him that I heard Nan and Grandad talking earlier. I know how upset they are. I also know that they are worried "now that social services are involved". What does that even mean? Will we be taken away?

"Is Mum in trouble?" Freddie asks me in a low voice, still not looking at me.

"I don't know."

"Is she in trouble for putting that bad drink in my bottle?" Freddie pauses, then adds, "Mum shouldn't have done that. It tasted horrible. It made me cough."

"I'm so sorry, Freddie," I say, my throat tightening. "I should've checked it."

"It was Mum's bottle," he replies matter-of-factly. "Why does she drink stuff like that? It's nasty."

"I don't know why she does," I tell him.

And I wish that she didn't.

"I told my teacher that Mummy is really sad," Freddie continues as his pencil moves frantically across the page. "I told my teacher that she shouts a lot and she cries."

"Why did you do that, Freddie?" I whisper.

He finally puts his pencil down and turns to me. His eyes are wide and his plump little cheeks are bright pink. He chews on his bottom lip thoughtfully.

"I told my teacher because I'm sad too," Freddie says at last. "I want Mummy to be like she used to be."

I can't stop them then. My tears are so strong that they are impossible to fight. I bend down and scoop Freddie into a tight hug, thrusting my face into his soft hair.

"I want that too, Freddie," I choke. "I want that too. So much."

Later that evening, Mum sits with me in Nan and Grandad's kitchen. It is just the two of us. She takes my hand in hers. Her skin feels dry and cool. I can barely stand to look at her face, but when I do it makes me want to cry all over again.

Mum looks so frail and hollow. Like someone has sucked all of the sparkle out of her. The dark rings under her eyes are much more prominent in the bright light and her skin has a sickly yellow hue to it.

"I'm so sorry," Mum whispers. "For everything."

"I'm sorry too," I say, and turn my head away, hardly able to stand it. But Mum squeezes my hand tighter – forcing me to look at her again.

"What on earth, Vee?" Mum asks. "What on earth are you sorry for?"

"For not checking that bottle ... For rushing. For talking to the social workers." I shiver. "This is all my fault."

"No. No," Mum says, her voice sharp. "This is *my* fault. All mine. And I told the social workers the same. You mustn't blame yourself."

"I thought you were better," I tell her. "I thought you weren't drinking any more."

"No – well." Mum takes a breath. "I am still drinking. A bit more than—" She shakes her head, not able to continue.

"You told me everything was going to be OK."

"I thought it would be," Mum says, her words sounding broken. "I'm sorry. I'm so, so sorry."

A silence falls between us. I can't speak. I actually don't know what to say any more and Mum seems so small in front of me, like she is shrinking all the time. I want to reach forward and hug her, but something holds me back.

Mum did this to us.

She lied.

She ruined everything.

Mum's head turns towards me, her eyes glistening with tears. She holds my gaze, her eyes steady, and sighs softly. "Vee – I'm an alcoholic. OK?" she says. "An alcoholic. I hate the word. I hate admitting it to myself, but there it is. I have an addiction. That means that I do bad stuff to feed my habit, like lie to you and pretend that I'm OK – when really I'm not."

"Have you had a drink today?" I ask sharply.

Mum releases my hand. She won't look me in the eye now. "I'm not here to talk about that," she says.

"Have you?" My voice is louder this time.

Mum nods reluctantly. "Yes. I had to. Just to get through this."

"But I don't understand. I don't get why you have to do this." My voice is wobbling now. "Why can't you stop for me and Freddie?"

"It's not as easy as that …"

"Was it Steve leaving?" I ask. "Is that what made you so unhappy?"

"No … No …" Mum rubs her face. "I mean, it didn't help. I probably seemed happier then, but I was still drinking. People call it social drinking, but I always had more than everyone else. Steve didn't like it. He tried to help me. He told me it was a problem, but I didn't listen …"

"But you always seemed so happy?" I say, confused. I picture Mum a year or so ago, laughing and joking with Steve.

"I was loud and the centre of attention," Mum says slowly. "That's what drinking helped me to be. I've been using it as a tool for too long – to help me be something I'm not. I've convinced myself that I need drink to get through the day … but in reality, it's killing me."

I think back to those days – to my loud, proud Mum. I always assumed she had everything under control. I never noticed her drinking much before. How could I have been so wrong?

"I – I thought you were so happy then. Confident," I whisper. "I admired you. I thought you were amazing."

"It's a mask. I'm not confident, not really," Mum admits. She half laughs – it sounds sharp and bitter. "I hardly even know who I am any more to be honest. I've been pretending for too long."

"So what now?" I ask. "What are you going to do?"

Mum looks at me. Her eyes are clear and fixed on mine. "I get better, Vee. That's what I do. I get help. I stop pretending that I can do this on my own. Your nan has booked me into a clinic. It's meant to be one of the top ..." Mum's voice drifts again before she adds, "It's my best chance."

"But what about us?" I say, my voice shaking. "What do we do?"

"You wait for me. You stay here with Nan and Grandad and wait for me to get better. And I will get better, Vee. I promise." Tears are flowing freely from Mum's eyes now. "Do you believe me? Do you believe me, Vee?"

I am flustered, unsure. "I – I dunno, Mum ... I want to. I really do ... but ..."

Mum reaches forward. Takes my hands in hers and squeezes them gently. "I promise I will try, Vee. For you. For Freddie. For us. I'll try. That's all I can do."

ELEVEN

A few days later, we're standing by the front door, all of us. Mum and Nan move down onto the path, and Nan clasps her car keys in her hand. I can tell Nan is nervous by the way she keeps jangling the keys in her hand, with tears dancing in her eyes. Behind me, Grandad grips my hand.

"It'll be OK, Violet," he says. "Your mum is stronger than you think. She will get through this."

The last few days have been so tough, really tough. I had to stay off school, but Nan says it was OK and that the school understood. It was more important that I got my "head together" and had some space to work through my feelings. I sat with Mum a lot. We didn't talk much – neither of us were up to that. Instead we watched

TV together and sometimes went for short walks. I tried not to say anything when I saw her drink from her bottle. Nan said it would take time for Mum to "ease out" of the habit, but even though I understand that now, I still hate it.

Yesterday we walked to the park with Freddie. Mum gripped my hand as we stood on the field together.

"I'll be home soon," Mum said. "And we'll come here again. Us three. It'll be different."

I tipped my head up to the sky, not sure what to say. I wanted to believe her. I really did. But this was so hard.

"We can bring your old kite!" Freddie said, suddenly excited. "Grandad has nearly fixed it. It'll be ready by the time you come home."

Mum froze for a second and then smiled. "My kite?" she said. "Seriously? He still has that thing? I used to love flying it over Gorse Hill – it was so beautiful."

"Can we do that together?" Freddie asked her.

"Yes, yes, we should." Mum squeezed my hand. "What do you think, Vee? Do you fancy that? Shall we do it when I'm better?"

I stared up at the clouds and imagined that beautiful kite darting among them. Suddenly it was the only thing I wanted to do.

"Yes," I said. "Yes, it sounds perfect."

And it really did.

But now it is time for Mum to go.

In the front garden, Mum is crouched on the ground, hugging Freddie tightly against her. When Mum stands up, I see the tears streaking down her face. Freddie slips back between me and Grandad and takes my hand. His hand is hot and sticky.

Mum steps forward and touches my cheek lightly. I lift my face to look at her, even though it is hard.

"Help look after Freddie, won't you?" Mum says. Her voice has a tiny wobble to it.

"I will ..." I tell her.

"This won't be long. I'll soon be home again." She swallows. "I – I'll soon be a mum again to you both."

"You've always been a mum," I say, and mean it.

Mum's hand flutters on my cheek. She holds my gaze for a moment and then a small smile slips onto her face. It is funny how much I have missed that. The smile lights her up totally.

"I love you, Vee," Mum whispers. "To the moon—"

"And back …" I finish.

We watch as Mum takes Nan's arm and the pair of them walk to the car. Mum doesn't look back, but I can see that her shoulders are shaking. I know she is crying. I squash Freddie's hand in mine.

"I don't want her to go," Freddie says.

"Neither do I," I whisper. "But Mum's going to get better."

We keep watching as she folds herself into the car and turns her face away from the window. She looks so small, like a frail child.

It is only as the car begins to pull away that Mum looks at us again. Her hand reaches up in a tiny wave but then suddenly stops. Instead she brings her hand up to her lips, and her fingers send us a gentle kiss. One soft, quick kiss in the air.

I know then that this isn't really goodbye.

This is about starting our new beginning.

I blow a kiss back to my beautiful brave mum.

And I finally believe her.

Our books are tested
for children and young people by
children and young people.

Thanks to everyone who consulted on
a manuscript for their time and effort in
helping us to make our books better
for our readers.